THE SOCIETY FOR THE PROTECTION OF ENDANGERED AND AWESOMELY RARE SPECIES

For Charlotte
J.B.

For Ida, my tiny, perfect tyrant
A.L.

A special thanks to design whizz Jamie Hammond

First published 2020 by Walker Books Ltd
87 Vauxhall Walk, London SE11 5HJ

2 4 6 8 10 9 7 5 3 1

This book has been typeset in Arapey

Printed and bound in China

British Library Cataloguing in Publication Data: a catalogue
record for this book is available from the British Library

ISBN 978-1-4063-8846-6
www.walker.co.uk

WALKER
BOOKS

FSC
www.fsc.org
MIX
Paper from
responsible sources
FSC® C008047

AGENTS OF THE WILD

OPERATION ICEBEAK

JENNIFER BELL & ALICE LICKENS

PROLOGUE

Eight-year-old Agnes Gamble stuck her head under her bed and considered how much her life had changed.

When she'd first come to stay with her uncle Douglas, he'd forbidden her from having any pets *and* refused her entirely reasonable offers to turn the spare room of their twenty-sixth-floor flat into a refuge for lost and injured birds.

Caring for the natural world, you see, was in Agnes's DNA. Her late parents (the famous botanists Ranulph and Azalea Gamble) had taught her all the important things she knew, like how to repair the nest of a red ovenbird; what kind of figs to feed a Bulmer's fruit bat, and the right way to treat stem rust fungus.

Douglas didn't appreciate that sort of thing.

"It'll only die," he'd told Agnes, after she'd given him a potted hydrangea for his birthday one year. "And anyway, there's no space for it in the kitchen. I want to get a new coffee machine."

Every birthday since, she'd given him a tie. It was kinder to plants.

But *now* Agnes had a secret.

Hidden under her bed, behind a tray of rare aloe seedlings she'd been incubating over winter, was a carefully folded uniform. It was made of waterproof, fireproof and mosquito-proof material and there was a small badge pinned to the chest pocket with the letters *S P E A R S* written on it.

"SPEARS," *you say? "Never heard of them!"*

Well, of course you haven't. **SPEARS** are the Society for the Protection of Endangered and Awesomely Rare Species, and they're **TOP SECRET**.

You probably haven't heard of the sparkle-muffin peacock spider either.

Or the pink fairy armadillo.

Or the red-lipped batfish.

And that's because they're all *awesomely rare,* and exactly the kind of species **SPEARS** tries to protect.

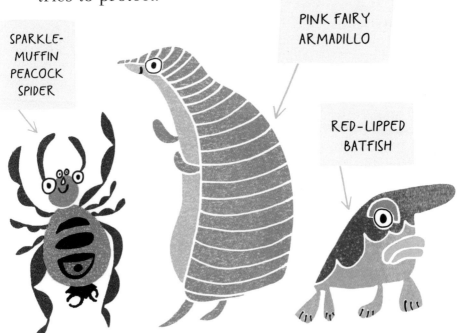

SPARKLE-
MUFFIN
PEACOCK
SPIDER

PINK FAIRY
ARMADILLO

RED-LIPPED
BATFISH

Agnes had been surprised by some of the plants and animals she'd encountered during her work for **SPEARS**, but then she'd only completed one mission so far, and she was still learning. She was now a permanent **SPEARS** field agent, working alongside her partner, Attie – a seriously impressive and impressively serious elephant shrew.

Whenever Agnes ran her fingers over the **SPEARS** badge on her uniform, she was reminded that she was now a part of something bigger, something that her parents – who had also been **SPEARS** agents – had been a part of too. She knew that if she and Attie could help protect the world's flora and fauna as they had, she'd be making them proud.

And so every morning Agnes crawled under her bed to check on her uniform, determined to be ready for whenever **SPEARS** might call...

CHAPTER ONE

There were strange noises coming from
the kitchen. Agnes sat bolt upright in bed,
knowing that it was long past midnight and
Uncle Douglas would have fallen asleep hours
ago. She listened carefully to the muffled
creaking and scratching. It sounded as if
someone was rummaging around.

Her curiosity building, she slipped on her hedgehog-shaped slippers, padded quietly out of her bedroom and ventured along the hallway towards the kitchen.

Passing the waste bin, Agnes noticed that her uncle had – once *again* – stuffed yesterday's newspaper into the wrong bin, so she fished it out and moved it into the recycling. The headline on the front page briefly caught her eye: MYSTERIOUS TREMORS FELT IN SCOTIA SEA. The Scotia Sea, she knew, was under the southern tip of South America. She hoped no wildlife had been affected.

She tiptoed past Douglas's bedroom door (she could hear him snoring) and into the shadowy kitchen, where she immediately discovered the cause of all the racket:

It was the refrigerator.

Or more precisely, it was something moving around *inside* the refrigerator.

Without hesitation, she gripped the door handle and yanked it open.

A small, four-legged animal with an elongated nose was standing on top of the butter dish. Its fur was chili-red on its head and jet-black everywhere else, except for two white rings around its eyes that made it look as if it was wearing spectacles.

"Attie?" Agnes exclaimed. Her **SPEARS** partner was easy to recognize, despite the unexpected place in which she'd found him.

He was dressed in a neatly ironed ice-blue **SPEARS** onesie which had a long, padded section for his tail, built-in gloves and a hood fitted with a transparent visor. "What are you *doing* in there?"

Attie's whiskers wiggled. "I'm trying to open the hidden passage behind this fridge, but it's proving rather difficult." A light flashed on the **SPEARS** communication pin fixed to his top pocket, which allowed Agnes to understand what he was saying. "**SPEARS** installed it a few weeks ago."

"A *hidden passage*?" Agnes knew that the organization had secret tunnels and bases all over the world, but she hadn't anticipated they would fit one in Uncle Douglas's apartment.

"There's a code that unlocks the door in the wall right behind the fridge," Attie explained, swapping around the different coloured grapes in a bowl. "I just can't quite–" there was a loud click "–aha, cracked it! Red, red, green, red, green, green. I should have known."

There was a secret grape code? Agnes quickly tried to commit it to memory as the back of the refrigerator slid away to reveal a dark corridor in the wall behind. A waft of cool air brushed past her, smelling of damp earth. "Where does it lead?"

"To an underground **SPEARS** equipment station on the other side of the city," Attie answered, rearranging the grapes back to their original positions. "We've been tasked with our second mission and we need to head there immediately."

Our second mission! Agnes whipped out her "Field Notes" journal and a ready-sharpened pencil from her pyjama pocket – she carried both with her at all times.

"What do we know so far?" she asked, turning to a clean page.

Right then, a chimp wearing identical pyjamas and hedgehog slippers to Agnes appeared inside the hidden passage. It squeezed past Attie, jumped out of the fridge and landed nimbly on the kitchen floor,

catching one of Uncle Douglas's ready meals in its hand.

"Ralph!" Careful not to jab the chimp with her pencil, Agnes gave him a hug. She'd grown fond of him while he'd been covering for her whenever she was away doing **SPEARS** training. Trained to only ever be seen from behind, Ralph was so good at mimicking Agnes's appearance that Uncle Douglas had never noticed the difference.

He beamed at her and then plodded off towards her bedroom with the ready meal tucked under his arm.

"He's probably in a hurry," Attie commented, reshuffling the contents of the fridge so there was space for Agnes to clamber in. "There's a new Cynthia Steelsharp documentary starting on TV in a few minutes and Ralph's a huge fan."

Agnes heard a twinge of disappointment in Attie's voice. Cynthia Steelsharp, she knew, was also one of *his* favourite animal experts. She'd won several awards for her studies of the planet's most endangered birds.

Attie grabbed a container of banana slices from the fridge (ingredients for his favourite pumpkin-seed-and-fried-banana sandwiches) and bounded into the hidden passage. Agnes returned her "Field Notes" journal and pencil to her pocket and crawled after him.

The dusty brick-lined tunnel beyond was so dark Agnes couldn't see where it ended, but after only a few metres, Attie stopped beside a large hole in the floor which seemed to narrow as it plunged deeper.

"This speed funnel will take us straight to the equipment station," he said, flicking his padded tail as he balanced on the funnel's edge. "I'll see you at the bottom." With the elegance of a kingfisher, he dived head first into the opening, slid round and round on his tummy and then disappeared into the hole at the bottom.

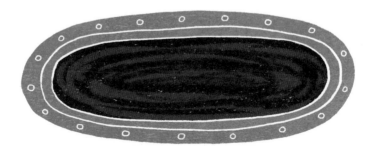

Agnes sat down and swung her legs into the funnel opening, trying to steady her nerves. She was doing important work for **SPEARS** now; she couldn't let herself be daunted by anything. Pushing off with her hands, she slipped forward, spiralled round and plunged into darkness. "Attie-e-e-!" she spluttered, whizzing along. "Where are weee go-ing?"

His reply echoed back to her. "An-tar-teee-ca!"

Agnes flinched. Had she heard him right?

A moment later, she left the tunnel and
landed on a soft straw mat in the corner
of a large cave. "Did you say *Antarctica*?"
she asked breathlessly. Her parents had
once adventured to the South Pole to study
Antarctic hair grass. Afterwards, they'd told
Agnes stories of a vast white wilderness,
home to specially adapted wildlife. It
had sounded incredible.

"That's right," Attie said, puffing up his chest. "**SPEARS** must think highly of us because Antarctica is a dangerous place, and they'd only send their best agents."

Marching through the cave (which was lit by millions of glowing railroad worms), Agnes glanced at his outfit. "Now I understand why you're wearing a onesie. It's to keep you warm."

"A *onesie?*" Attie jerked his head. "**SPEARS** agents do not wear *onesies*, Agent Gamble! This is a watertight thermal bodysuit, designed using technology inspired by Antarctic silverfish. You'll be wearing one too, soon."

As he walked faster, muttering "onesie" under his breath and shaking his head, Agnes considered how his suit might work.

SPEARS technology was based on the science of the natural world and Agnes had a vague memory of her dad teaching her that Antarctic silverfish produce their own natural antifreeze in order to survive in sub-zero temperatures. Perhaps when underwater, the thermal bodysuit used antifreeze too.

The cave soon widened into an enormous space filled with peculiar vehicles. Agnes spied a dragoncopter and an albatross glider like those she'd ridden on her last mission, but also a hovercraft with spindly insect antennae, a sleek cheetah-shaped motorbike and a submarine covered in glittering fish scales. Attie stopped beside a vessel shaped like a giant toad with a lumpy transparent back.

"This is our means of transport for the journey to Antarctica," Attie announced,

gesturing at the toad-shaped craft. "It's capable of travelling on land and in water, so we call it an omnifrog." He spread his claws over a scanner on the outer wall and, with a hiss, a set of steps unfolded from the omnifrog's mouth.

Agnes understood where the vessel's name had come from. Frogs were *amphibians*, which meant that like the omnifrog, they were specially adapted to survive in water and on land.

Inside, the omnifrog was spotlessly clean and smelled of lemon disinfectant. Agnes found a child-sized thermal bodysuit hanging from a peg and wriggled into it as she listened to Attie's instructions. Pointing with his tail, he showed her where their new colour-coded equipment was stored, which she would need to learn about during the journey.

Taking the chair beside Attie, Agnes fumbled with her seat belt, a mixture of nerves and excitement bubbling inside her. In front of them was a control panel crammed with various buttons, levers and switches. Attie turned a dial, and, with a loud croak, the engine of the omnifrog started. The walls of the vessel shook as it sank below the surface, sending a cloud of bubbles swirling over the glass panels in the roof. Agnes could see a dark tunnel up ahead.

"We've received this message from **SPEARS** HQ," Attie said, flicking a switch.

A screen lit up, showing the image of a portly turkey sitting with his wings folded across his belly and a severe expression on his wrinkly pink face. It was Commander Phil, the fearless leader of **SPEARS**.

"Agents Attenborough and Gamble, I have an urgent assignment for you," the Commander said in a gruff voice that made his throat wobble. "We have received a Level *Ten* distress call from an underwater **SPEARS** outpost in Antarctica." His image moved to the left-hand side of the screen as a map appeared on the right-hand side. It displayed the jagged ice-white continent of Antarctica with a flashing red cross in the Weddell Sea, north-west of the Antarctic Peninsula.

A Level Ten distress call? Agnes's chest tightened as she glanced at Attie. Level Ten was code for: IMMEDIATE DANGER.

"Three **SPEARS** agents are stationed at the outpost," the Commander continued. "The nature of their distress call is unclear because their communications equipment has been damaged, so it is even more vital that you reach them quickly to learn what's happened." His chest feathers ruffled as he added, "Our **SPEARS** family is in trouble and we need *you*. Good luck."

The image on the screen faded and a long reel of paper emerged from a slit in the control panel. Agnes read it as fast as she could.

MISSION NAME:
OPERATION ICEBEAK

MISSION TYPE:
Aid and investigate

ASSIGNED EQUIPMENT:
Omnifrog, trinoculars, supersonic otter sled and telescopic giraffe stilts

CHAPTER TWO

Goosebumps prickled the backs of Agnes's arms as a pod of enormous fin whales swam over the glass-bubbled roof of the omnifrog. She watched their pale grey undersides glide majestically through the water, marvelling at how the second largest animal on Earth was able to move so fast.

"Incredible, aren't they?" Attie said, gawping up at them. He tapped his hairy little foot on the copy of *The **SPEARS** Guide To Cold-Weather Injuries* that lay open on the floor. "But we'd better continue testing each other. Let me see... Can you name four signs of hypothermia?"

Agnes pointed to Attie's head, mouth and chest. "Sleepiness, slurred speech, slow breathing and weak pulse," she recited. To survive in Antarctica they would need to look out for each other, so they'd been studying throughout their long journey. "I also know the best way to treat frostbite, how to prevent snow blindness and how to detect cracks in the snow so we don't fall into a crevasse." She pushed her shoulders back and lifted her chin. "You can count on me."

Attie nodded but Agnes could tell he was worried because his tail hadn't stopped twitching since they'd set off. This mission was important, and they'd need to overcome the hazards of the environment if they wanted to succeed.

Just then, the control panel began beeping. Attie's ears pricked up. "We must be arriving. Prepare to dock!"

Emerging in the distance was a tall knobbly structure that looked like an enormous pink coral rising up from the seabed.

The underwater outpost.

As they glided closer, Agnes saw that each gnarled bump on the building was actually a transparent pod filled with sea-water. A variety of marine animals – from black

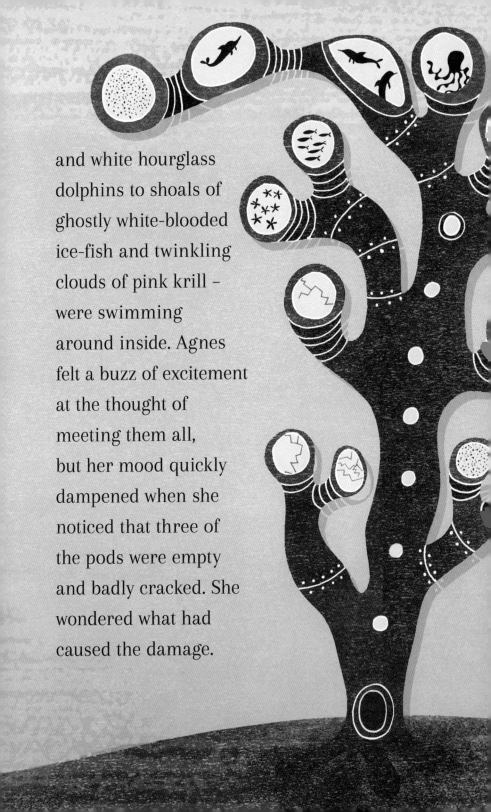

and white hourglass dolphins to shoals of ghostly white-blooded ice-fish and twinkling clouds of pink krill – were swimming around inside. Agnes felt a buzz of excitement at the thought of meeting them all, but her mood quickly dampened when she noticed that three of the pods were empty and badly cracked. She wondered what had caused the damage.

"Remember: the agents we're about to meet are relying on us to help them," Attie said, smoothing down his thermal bodysuit as they waited by the omnifrog door, "so it's important we make a confident first impression."

The floor jolted as the omnifrog connected to a port in the underwater outpost. With a long creak, both sets of doors slid open.

Agnes blinked as they were greeted by a mountain of shaggy brown hair with a leathery black nose and two curved horns. She racked her brains for hairy animals over six feet tall that fitted that description and realized she could only be looking at one species: the American bison.

"Welcome to Outpost Twenty-Two," the bison said, in an unexpectedly soft voice. "I'm Agent Wallace, but feel free to call me Wally."

Agnes stepped forward. "Nice to meet you, Wally. I'm Agent—"

But before she could finish, she tripped over her new thermal boots and slipped right between Wally's two front legs. Muttering an apology, she tried to scramble back up – only to lose her footing and headbutt Wally in the nose!

A booming *"AITCHOO!"* was followed by a loud *SPLAT*. When Agnes finally righted herself, Attie was wiping congealed Bison snot off his thermal bodysuit.

"I'm so sorry," she mumbled, feeling her cheeks go red.

Attie twitched his snout. "What Agent Gamble *meant* to say," he told Wally, hopping over a puddle of snot, "is that it's a pleasure to meet you. I'm Agent Attenborough."

A boy of Agnes's age stepped out from behind Agent Wallace and shook Attie's paw. There was seaweed sticking out of his curly black hair and perched on his shoulder was a chameleon wearing four miniature thermal boots over its bodysuit. "I'm Wally's partner, Agent Rahul Kapoor, and this is Agent Dita, who transferred here from another **SPEARS** outpost to help us. We're all so glad you've come."

The chameleon ogled Agnes with her jewelled eyes, which moved independently of each other like two marbles floating in water. Her scaly green skin had orange, white and yellow stripes and there was a cone-shaped protrusion on her head, characteristic of one particular species: the veiled chameleon. Agnes had never met one in real life. She gave her a broad smile.

Rahul turned inside. "We must show you both to the briefing pod immediately so we can explain what's going on. Wally and I will give you a tour of the outpost on the way."

Attie scurried along at Wally's side as Rahul led them all into the building. The narrow, winding passageways of the outpost were puddled with water and smelled bitter and salty like seaweed.

"I'm sorry I wasn't able to warn you before you tripped up, Agent Gamble," Dita told Agnes. Her long padded tail swayed back and forth as she adjusted herself on Rahul's shoulder. "I should have seen it coming."

Rahul patted Dita on the head. "I've told you before. Just because you have panoramic vision, it doesn't mean everyone expects you to be on high alert all the time. Don't worry so much." He whispered aside to Agnes, "Dita finds it difficult to relax."

Agnes gazed longingly at Attie, wondering if he might ever sit on her shoulder.

"Well, just mind how you go," Dita said, jumpily. "It's slippery around here."

Heeding Dita's advice, Agnes tried to concentrate on where she placed her feet. She didn't want to headbutt anyone else in the nose.

"Outpost Twenty-Two is used as a treatment centre for sick marine life," Wally explained, ahead. "We admit patients with all kinds of problems, from injuries caused by fishing boats to exhaustion resulting from a lack of ice to rest on."

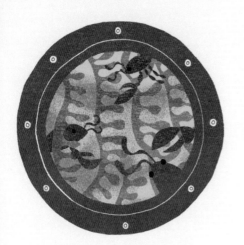 

Agnes passed door after door, each one sliding open into the pods she had seen from the outside. After glancing at the medical notes about each pod's occupant, she peeked through the viewing windows. In one, an octopus was sitting comfortably on a bed of sand, recovering after having a plastic bag removed from its tentacles. In another, a family of lobsters were scuttling around through a forest of dark green kelp after being treated for cracked pincers.

"Antarctica is experiencing more dramatic changes than anywhere else on the planet because of global warming," Wally continued. "Most of the animals we treat have problems caused by rising sea-temperatures."

Thanks to her **SPEARS** training, Agnes knew all about the destructive effects of global warming. It posed an even bigger threat to the environment than the shady characters named in the most recent edition of the **SPEARS** *Handbook of Known Enemies.*

Rahul pressed his finger against a window, pointing to where a group of sea snails were rolling around on a shallow tray coated in a sticky yellow balm. "This is the snail spa, where crustaceans can get their shells coated in anti-acid balm to stop them from dissolving."

"Dissolving?" Agnes was horrified. "That's terrible."

Rahul sighed. "There's so much carbon dioxide in the water now that it acts like acid. Wally and I came up with a formula which helps protect them."

Agnes's heart sank lower as they continued through the building, learning about all the different ailments the patients had. Once again she felt thankful to be part of an organization like **SPEARS**, doing what they could to help. "And there's just the three of you working here?" she asked, amazed that they managed to care for so many creatures between them.

"We're trained professionals," Rahul said, standing straighter, "but there are so many new patients coming in we're run off our feet. That's why we need *your* help with this latest situation. We just aren't able to leave the outpost to investigate what's going on ourselves."

On his shoulder, Dita suddenly tensed. "Watch out! I can see—"

But before she finished, the building started shaking. Heavy vibrations travelled up Agnes's legs, shuddering every bone in her body. She dropped to the floor and threw her arms protectively over her head. "What's going on?"

Crouching beside her, Rahul raised his voice above the deep rumbling. "This is the reason we sent the distress call! These tremors have been happening several times a day for the past week, causing serious damage to the outpost. We've checked for local seismic activity and these aren't earthquakes. Whatever's causing them, it isn't natural!"

Agnes heard the water in the treatment pods sloshing around and the patients wailing in alarm. This must be the cause of the smashed pods she'd seen on the outside of the building. She recalled the headline on Uncle Douglas's newspaper: MYSTERIOUS TREMORS FELT IN SCOTIA SEA. The Scotia Sea wasn't too far away from their current location...

"We need you and Attie to find out about and stop whatever it is that is causing the quakes," Wally said, his fur trembling. "We're not sure how many more the outpost can take before it's destroyed completely!"

CHAPTER THREE

Agnes planted her boots in the snow and checked the thermometer attached to her padded sleeve. The air was a freezing minus twenty degrees but in her thermal bodysuit, she felt toasty warm.

She gazed around at the dazzlingly white Antarctic landscape, unable to believe she was really there. Where the land fractured into the sea, wedge-shaped icebergs soared up through the dark water, glowing turquoise-blue under the surface. For such a harsh environment, it was incredibly beautiful.

Opening her "Field Notes" journal, she read through her list of *Important Things to Remember When You're in Antarctica*. "Did you scrub your suit clean before we left the omnifrog?" she asked Attie. The Antarctic ecosystem was so fragile they had to be careful not to contaminate the area with any foreign bodies they might have picked up elsewhere.

"*Three* times to be sure," he replied. "And I packed extra supplies in case we get caught in a snowstorm. We can't be over-prepared." The snow was already so deep, he'd attached a pair of telescopic giraffe stilts to his boots so that he wasn't completely buried as they trekked. "Let's begin our investigation right away. We've got to stop those tremors."

Agnes shivered as she considered what might happen if the outpost was destroyed. All those sick animals would have nowhere to go to get help... It was too horrible to imagine.

Unshouldering his pack, Attie retrieved a pair of stripy black-and-white binoculars –

except, unlike binoculars, the lenses resembled rainbow-swirly bubbles and were mounted on stalks that moved independently of each other, like Dita's eyes.

Trinoculars, Agnes guessed. She remembered reading the name in their mission briefing.

"I had to pass a two-week training course to learn how to use these," Attie said proudly, lifting the trinoculars to his eyes. Agnes tried not to giggle; it looked like he was wearing a pair of googly-eye glasses.

"They utilize zebra mantis-shrimp technology to scan *through* the ice, right down to the seabed," he explained. "If anything down there is causing those tremors, I should be able to see it."

While Attie searched, Agnes surveyed the area for clues and spotted several hefty stone boulders scattered across the shoreline. Her gaze moved elsewhere, but then in the corner of her eye, she glimpsed one of the boulders *moving...*

"I can't see anything suspicious," Attie announced, lowering the trinoculars. "Let's continue trekking and try again in another spot."

Agnes had an idea. "Before we move on, why don't we ask the local wildlife? Someone might have seen something that could help explain what's going on."

As they approached the shoreline, the

"boulders" were shifting around, grunting. Agnes took note of their thick grey-brown skin, angled flippers and the bulbous growth on their noses, and identified them quickly: southern elephant seals, the biggest and heaviest species of seal in the world.

She tapped the **SPEARS** communication pin on her chest to double-check it was working. "Hello there!" she called. "We work for **SPEARS**. I was hoping we could ask you a few questions?"

The closest seal – a bull, who was easily the size of a small car – yawned, revealing a huge pink mouth and pointed teeth on either side of his jaw. "Maybe," he bellowed, in a voice like a foghorn, making Attie's ears flap back, "but I doubt you have anything we want in return."

It wasn't the response Agnes had hoped for. Elephant seals, she knew, were notoriously greedy animals who spent the majority of their lives in the water, hunting for food.

"Perhaps you'd be interested in a trade?" she suggested, thinking quickly. She considered what she and Attie were carrying that might appeal to the seal. Apart from their **SPEARS** equipment, the only thing they'd brought with them were their food supplies. "In exchange for answering my questions, we could give you some banana slices."

Attie shot Agnes a look of panic, as if to say, "*No! We need those to make our sandwiches!*" But the offer had already been made.

The seal lifted a hairy eyebrow. "Hmmm... I've never eaten bananas before." It licked its lips. "You have a deal."

"Great." Agnes understood Attie's reluctance to give away their food, but if

they got some useful information in return, it would be worth it. Attie unpacked the bananas from his rucksack with a sour expression on his face and handed them over.

"So," Agnes began, opening her "Field Notes" journal, "question one: have you felt any tremors recently?"

"Of course," the elephant seal replied. "Everything feels like it's shaking when I move."

Agnes's pencil hovered over the page. "No," she said, trying to be patient. "These tremors would be in the ground or sea – caused by something other than your own weight."

The elephant seal thought for a moment. "I don't think so. Unless ... there are waves on the water. Do you mean those?"

Attie slapped a paw against his face. "No, not the waves! Oh, this is useless." He closed his pack, scowling at Agnes. "Let's ask a creature with some sense. We don't have time or bananas to waste."

They left the elephant seal tucking into their bananas and ventured further inland, Attie marching huffily through the snow on his stilts. Agnes couldn't help feeling as if she'd let him down. She'd thought it was a good idea to trade with the seal, but she hadn't even asked Attie's opinion first. And that was what being partners was all about.

Soon, a large bird glided down beside them. Noting the incredible length of its black and white wings, Agnes decided it was a wandering albatross – they had the largest wingspan of any living bird and spent weeks in the sky without landing.

The albatross tipped its head as it flew alongside them. "How do you do?" it asked. "I was just wondering if you've heard anything more about BOI? The last time I flew close to the ice, I overheard a pair of crabs talking about it. They were very excited."

"BOI?" Agnes repeated. "No, sorry. I've never heard of it." She jotted the letters down in her "Field Notes" journal just in case they might be connected to the tremors.

The albatross fluffed the feathers on its shoulders. "Never mind. I'll ask again in a few weeks." With the tiniest flick of its wings, it soared higher and became a distant dot in the cloudy sky.

It grew colder as Agnes and Attie continued their trek. The wind picked up, carrying with it thick drifts of snow, which made it difficult to see more than a few metres ahead. After interviewing a couple of Antarctic midges – who had burrowed under the snow to survive the cold temperatures, and knew nothing – they were feeling pretty hopeless.

"We've made no progress," Attie admitted, scanning under the ice with the trinoculars again. "How are we meant to stop the tremors if we don't know what's causing them?"

Agnes thought carefully. Investigations required patience. Once you'd gathered the clues, you had to piece them all together like a puzzle. The answers would be there, if they just looked hard enough.

Squinting through the heavy snowfall, she spotted a set of fresh footprints leading into the distance. Thanks to her **SPEARS** training, she could tell that the prints had been made by a two-legged creature with narrow three-toed feet who now and again had stopped walking, plonked itself on its belly and tobogganed along over the snow.

And Agnes knew of only one animal who moved across Antarctica using that technique. She followed the trail into the distance and caught sight of a mottled black and white blob *waddling* over a hill. "Penguin!" she shouted triumphantly.

Attie checked through the trinoculars. "Well spotted, Agent Gamble! Let's see what it can tell us."

Penguin facts swirled through Agnes's head as they trudged over. She knew there were eighteen species in the world. Four lived in Antarctica, and another four lived on the islands around Antarctica – so it could be any one of those.

Her spirits lifted as she

got closer and saw that the penguin had distinctive white rings around its eyes, characteristic of Adélie penguins. They were Agnes's favourite species because, like her, they were very small, very brave and very clumsy. This particular Adélie, however, was slightly unusual. Its darker feathers were actually brown, not black, and, most curious of all, it was wearing a silver bow tie fixed around its neck, with a green flashing light in the middle.

"Excuse me?" Agnes called, waving. Attie bent his knees and sprang up and down on his stilts, trying to get the penguin's attention.

It must have been an odd sight, but the penguin trundled on without so much as a glance in their direction.

"Hello!" Agnes tried again, lifting her voice above the roar of the wind.

But the penguin continued to ignore her. It had a dazed look in its eyes, as if it was dreaming.

Attie snorted, making his visor steam up. "How rude!"

"Perhaps it can't hear us," Agnes suggested, knowing that penguins spent a lot of time underwater. "It might have an ear infection." But she still thought this penguin's behaviour was strange. There was a chance it might have encountered a human before, but she doubted very much that it would ever have seen a jumping elephant shrew in a onesie – and it wasn't even surprised!

Refusing to give up, they tailed the penguin up a hill. When they got to the very top, Agnes drew in her breath. An entire colony of black Adélie penguins were huddled in the valley below. They sat in pairs, each couple guarding a carefully organized pile of stones – a nest. Agnes thought it was strange to see them so far inland; they normally built their nests on the shoreline. And they were all wearing silver bow ties...

In the middle of the colony was a tent so enormous it could have been used as a wedding marquee, and standing beside it, a human figure. Perhaps, Agnes thought, she and Attie would find answers there.

CHAPTER FOUR

Careful not to disturb the penguins' nests, Agnes and Attie weaved through the colony towards the huge tent. The ground was covered in sticky penguin poop, which Agnes had read about. It was called *guano* and smelled of rotting shrimp. She was glad the stench couldn't penetrate her thermal suit, or else she might have fainted.

The penguins chatted away to each other as Agnes passed, but whenever she tried to engage them in conversation, they swiftly turned their heads and ignored her.

"I say, this white stuff is frightfully cold," one Adélie commented as it wiggled its bottom into a pile of snow.

"I quite agree," another chirped. "How very bothersome that it's everywhere."

"And have you seen this?" another asked, waving a flipper in front of its beak. "I can see my breath in the air!"

Agnes studied the penguins carefully. There was obviously something very wrong with them. Opening her "Field Notes" journal, she started a list of things that she found curious about them, including their unusual nesting site, their worrying behaviour and those silver bow ties.

The human figure standing by the tent, they soon discovered, was a tall woman with a mound of perfectly coiffured copper hair. She was dressed in a belted tangerine-orange quilted jacket and knee-high boots.

"Hello there!" she hollered as Agnes and Attie approached. Her smooth voice was somehow familiar. "It's so nice to have unexpected visitors! Please, come on in!"

Attie hesitated. "I don't believe it," he whispered, steadying himself against Agnes's leg. "Is that who I think it is?"

Agnes dusted her visor clean of snowflakes so she could see properly.

She gasped. It couldn't be...
Cynthia Steelsharp?!

Agnes had only ever seen the rare-bird researcher on TV, but Cynthia Steelsharp's slim face and trademark hairstyle were unmistakable.

Attie pushed his hood and visor back. "Goodness! I hadn't expected to see you here, Miss Steelsharp."

"I go where the animals are," Steelsharp said cheerily, flapping open the door of her tent so they could enter.

The interior was luxuriously furnished with deep-pile rugs and cosy velvet sofas. There were cabinets displaying books and antiques, and the warm air smelled of wood smoke. "Please, take a seat." She ushered them over to a long wooden table topped with a stained-glass lamp.

Attie unfastened his stilts and placed

them by the door before bounding over. "What an honour to see where you work," he commented, gazing around. "It's lovely."

Agnes wasn't so sure. Half hidden behind a table, she spotted a generator pumping black fumes into a transparent plastic tube which led outside. It wasn't the kind of thing you'd use if you were taking care not to contaminate the environment, which left Agnes very confused.

"You're both from **SPEARS**," Steelsharp remarked, her wide green eyes flicking to the badge on Attie's thermal bodysuit. "I know a little about the organization, but I've never had the pleasure of meeting any of its representatives."

Attie's whiskers quivered excitedly. "I'm Agent Attenborough and this is my partner,

Agent Gamble. We're investigating the recent tremors in the area. I don't suppose you know anything about them?"

"Only that they've caused havoc with my equipment." Steelsharp gestured towards a stack of containers crammed with broken computer parts, including two which were, Agnes noticed, filled with silver bow ties. Beside them on a desk were maps, stacks of paperwork, an overflowing ashtray, a gold bullion paperweight and a calendar. A date twelve days from now was ringed in red and marked with the word AUCTION.

AUCTION

"Are you here studying the Adélies?" Agnes asked, curious to hear what Steelsharp had to say about their behaviour. "They're all wearing your bow ties."

Steelsharp's neck tensed. "Yes. I've been fitting the birds with those ... err, tracking devices, so I can observe their movements. They're acting strangely."

"Well, if anyone can understand why, it's you," Attie said, gazing admiringly up at his idol. Agnes wondered if all thoughts of their mission had left his mind; he looked completely star-struck. "I wonder, if it's not too much trouble," he said, fiddling with the zip of his suit, "would I be able to get a picture with you?"

"Of course," Steelsharp purred. "Anything for a fan."

Agnes helped Attie search through his pack to find the camera they'd packed earlier (in case they'd discovered any tremor-related evidence that they needed to photograph).

"Those look intriguing." Steelsharp pointed to the trinoculars Attie had placed on the table.

Grinning, he demonstrated their bubble-shaped lenses. "**SPEARS** technology. They allow me to see right through the ice."

"*Through* the ice?" Her eyes glittered. "Very impressive indeed."

After Agnes had taken *several* pictures of Attie and Steelsharp together (one serious, one laughing, one with Steelsharp and Attie pulling baboon faces),

she helped him repack his rucksack. All
the while, Attie bombarded Steelsharp with
questions about her career, his ears twitching
with interest at her answers.

Wind buffeted the tent walls, making
the canvas sides flap noisily. "It sounds like
the wind's growing stronger," Agnes said,
remembering the warnings given in the cold-
weather guide. "We should probably head
back to the outpost in case a storm's coming."

Attie nodded, although Agnes saw the
sides of his mouth pulling down. She knew
he'd much rather stay there and talk to
Steelsharp than venture outside again. As he
refastened his stilts and zipped up his hood,
he quizzed Steelsharp about everything from
the structure of golden eagle nests to the size
of ostrich eggs.

Agnes took one last look around the TV presenter's tent. She found it strange that she couldn't see any equipment that she recognized. She knew enough about research trips to know that all you really needed were notebooks, cameras, tripods, camera traps, pencils, a year's supply of trail mix and enough clothing to keep you warm when sitting very still for long periods of time. But Steelsharp had none of those things. It got Agnes thinking.

"Until we meet again," Attie said, shaking Steelsharp's hand.

She flashed him a gleaming white smile. "Good luck with your investigation."

Outside, the snow was falling more heavily and was as thick underfoot as four pillows piled on top of each other. Agnes had to wipe her visor clean every few steps. "Did you think there was anything strange about Miss Steelsharp?" she asked, delicately. "I couldn't see any evidence to suggest she was actually studying those penguins. My instincts tell me that there's more to her than meets the eye."

Attie snorted. "Nonsense. Miss Steelsharp is a world-renowned expert. Anyway, the last time you trusted your instincts, we ended up trading away our only bananas to an elephant seal. Perhaps you should trust *me* this time?"

Agnes studied her feet. Attie was probably right. He was also probably hungry. What was she thinking? She shook her head and plodded on.

From the comfort of her warm tent, Cynthia Steelsharp poured herself some hot cocoa and stood slurping it as she watched the two agents make their way across the ice. She tapped the sides of her mug, deep in thought. Once the small rat-creature and nosey little girl were over the hill and out of sight of the penguin colony, she shouted to the nearest bird, a brown-feathered Adélie. "You. Beak Brain. Send a coded message to my *assistant* at the outpost. I want those trinoculars snatched; they'll come in useful for our search."

The penguin had an empty look in its eyes as it stood up. It placed one webbed foot in front of the other, wobbled and swung round to face Cynthia's tent.

"No, you flat-footed goon!" She grabbed the penguin by the shoulders and spun it back around. "The radio is *that* way."

The penguin waddled off into the blizzard, obeying her command without question.

Steelsharp retreated into her tent, tightening her jaw and muttering under her breath, "Erg, I *hate* penguins."

CHAPTER FIVE

Very early the following morning, Agnes and Attie were in the omnifrog discussing their investigation over breakfast.

Agnes slurped down the last of her almond-milk porridge and rested her spoon in her empty bowl. "I've marked on a map where we searched yesterday, so we don't use the trinoculars on the same area twice," she said cheerfully, eager to make a success of their second day.

Attie sniffed experimentally at the sandwich in front of him. With no bananas available, he'd filled his two slices of bread with mushy green kelp bran. "My guess is the tremors are being caused by something very big and very powerful," he said, lifting the bread to his lips. "If we keep searching, we should find it." He took a small bite of the sandwich, scrunched up his long nose and hastily put it down. Agnes felt a pang of guilt, knowing it was her fault he couldn't eat his favourite food.

While Agnes collected their dirty dishes, Attie gathered their supplies from the equipment shelves in the omnifrog. Opening the striped black-and-white case that contained the trinoculars, he frowned.

"What's the matter?" Agnes asked.

"They're ... *gone*," he replied, flashing her the empty case. "Are you sure you put them back in the right place yesterday?"

"Positive."

He scratched his head. "So then what could have happened to them?" His tail twitched as he began checking through the other cases and containers. "We need to find them; they're essential to our investigation!"

Agnes joined the search, opening all the boxes on the higher shelves that Attie couldn't reach. Her stomach knotted. After accidentally headbutting Wally, gambling away Attie's bananas and now this ... she was beginning to feel like she wasn't the ace **SPEARS** partner she'd hoped to be.

She got to her knees to check underneath the supersonic otter sled (a sleek brown vehicle, capable of travelling at high speed across ice) and noticed a trail of wet patches shining on the floor. They led from the equipment shelves to the omnifrog door. "Look here," she said, studying the tracks. "Someone else has been in here without permission. Do you think the trinoculars were *stolen*?"

Attie scurried to the door and peered into the corridor. "It's certainly possible, but there are too many animal prints out there to identify which might belong to a thief. They all lead in the same direction, to the outpost canteen."

The canteen looked a bit like a school lunch hall with rows of long rocky tables, and specially adapted seats designed for all kinds of different marine animals. A huge pool in the middle of the room catered for the water-dwelling creatures and in one wall, floor to ceiling windows looked out into the dark ocean.

Agent Wallace, wearing the biggest hairnet Agnes had ever seen, loomed behind a serving counter, dishing out seaweed waffles and lichen granola to a queue of patients being fussed over by Rahul. Dita sat on a side table, picking up and distributing cutlery with her long sticky blue tongue, which shot in and out of her mouth in the blink of an eye.

"Let's split up and ask the diners," Attie suggested. "Someone might have noticed something."

Agnes scanned the room. A group of chubby, five-armed starfish were clinging high up to the canteen wall. They were coral-red on top with pink undersides covered in lots of small tube feet. Thinking they probably had the best vantage point, Agnes went over to question them. But as she crossed the canteen floor, she spotted something else.

Twirling around in the water outside was an enormous tentacled creature with purple-red skin. Agnes identified it with a gasp. It was a colossal squid, one of the great giants of the marine world. She knew they had the largest eyes in the animal kingdom – over thirty centimetres in diameter! If anyone had seen anything suspicious, it would be a creature with peepers that huge.

"Excuse me," she said, tapping lightly on the glass.

The squid's head wobbled. "Hello? Is someone there?" It waved its tentacles and shot forward, bumping into the side of the outpost. "Ouch!"

"Oh no!" Agnes exclaimed. "Are you all right? I didn't mean to startle you."

"It isn't your fault," the squid

said, tiredly. "I'm very old and my eyesight isn't what it used to be. My name's Haruki. I'm trying to find the eye-test pod. Is this it?"

"I'm afraid not," Agnes replied, hoping Haruki hadn't hurt himself too badly. "This is the canteen."

His tentacles drooped. "Silly me. I swim here every year from the southern tip of New Zealand for an eye test, you see. Normally I take a nap as soon as I arrive in a comfy ancient shipwreck near by, but on this occasion I didn't have time. Now I'm feeling rather disorientated."

Before Agnes could offer to help, the water filled with ripples and Haruki's head and tentacles started juddering. The canteen floor trembled as a deep, loud rumble reverberated through the outpost.

Over by the serving counter, Dita's skin changed from green to red. "It's happening again!" she cried, her eyes swivelling frantically in all directions. "Everyone, take cover!"

Flying waffle pieces filled the air as diners abandoned their breakfast and took shelter beneath the tables or in the pool. Agent Wallace leapfrogged across the serving

counter and gathered several leopard seal pups under his squashy belly for protection, while Rahul scooped a family of snails into his arms and crawled under a stool.

"Quick – get to safety!" Agnes told Haruki.

The squid spluttered a reply, but Agnes's attention was suddenly drawn by something else: a tiny crack had appeared in the glass of the canteen pod.

The window trembled and gave a high-pitched squeal as a spider's web of fractures spread across it and water started to bubble through the gaps. Agnes's heart was in her mouth, knowing it might shatter at any moment. Searching for a solution, she remembered the group of starfish huddled near the ceiling. "Hello over there!" she called, cupping her hands around her lips. "We need your help! Can you use your tube feet to seal this window?"

The starfish turned in her direction but as they had no mouths, Agnes's communication pin couldn't translate any speech. Instead, the starfish communicated by spelling words with their arms. They jostled around to spell out *WE TRY* and crawled at top speed towards the shattering

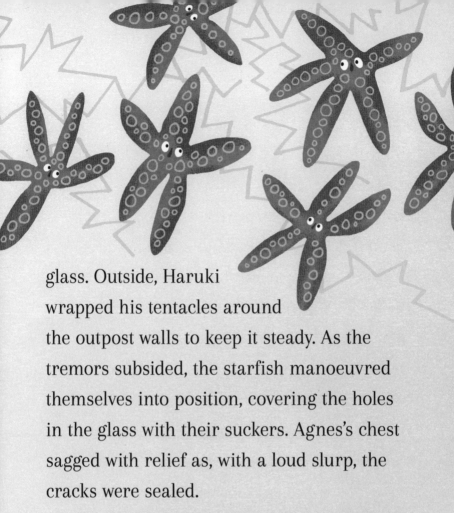

glass. Outside, Haruki
wrapped his tentacles around
the outpost walls to keep it steady. As the
tremors subsided, the starfish manoeuvred
themselves into position, covering the holes
in the glass with their suckers. Agnes's chest
sagged with relief as, with a loud slurp, the
cracks were sealed.

"Excellent thinking," Attie said, scurrying
to her side. "Once we've evacuated the
canteen, the glass can be repaired from the
outside and the starfish can safely let go."

Agnes watched in dismay as the diners

ran, scuttled and slid out of the room. "Yes, but I didn't get a chance to quiz anyone about the missing trinoculars, and without them we can't locate what's causing all this!"

"Then we'll just have to split up and interview everyone at the outpost," Attie decided. "You can start with the patients in the south and west wings; I'll speak to those in the north and east." He rubbed his whiskers. "I've been wondering about this possible thief: do you think they've stolen the trinoculars in order to sabotage our investigation?"

Agnes blinked. "Why would anyone want to do that?"

"I don't know," Attie replied, studying the departing crowd with his beady eyes. "That's what you and I need to find out."

CHAPTER SIX

Later that same morning, Agnes perched
on a damp stool inside a large, oval-shaped
treatment pod and opened her "Field Notes"
journal. The room featured a massive pool
at one end and smelled vaguely minty.
She'd seen on the schedule that Wally was
expecting a whale for a regular dental
hygienist appointment, but she didn't know
which species. She flicked a few water
droplets off the page and read back through
her notes. It had been a busy few hours.

OPERATION ICEBEAK

by Agnes Gamble (**SPEARS** Field Agent)

UPDATE:

Interviewing the patients of **SPEARS** Outpost Twenty-Two has been a challenging process. Most animals are receiving treatment in pools, so I have had to swim or snorkel into their pods to ask questions. I hope that wherever Agent Attenborough is, his interviews are going well and he has learned something useful. The idea that there might be someone aboard the outpost trying to disrupt our investigation makes me nervous.

INTERVIEWS

SUBJECT: Yeti crab (*Kiwa Hirsuta*)

NAME: Ansel

NOTES: Ansel is a rare species of crustacean with silky blond hairs all over his pincers, making him look fluffy. He has been admitted to the outpost for a hearing test.

> ME: Have you seen anyone acting suspiciously in the outpost?

> ANSEL: Not in the outpost, no. But a few days ago, you won't believe it, I saw a group of smartly dressed Adélies wearing bow ties! They were diving far deeper than normal, too. I did wonder what on earth they were up to...?

SUBJECT: Starfish (*Odontaster Validus*)
NAME: Sydney
NOTES: Sydney is one of a family of starfish who saved the glass of the outpost canteen from shattering after a particularly nasty tremor. As she has no mouth, the only way she could answer my questions was by spelling words with her arms.

ME: Other than myself and Agent Attenborough, did you notice anyone leaving the omnifrog this morning?

SYDNEY: NO

ME: Can you tell me about anything unusual happening in the local area?

SYDNEY: BOI.

The interview answers swirled through Agnes's mind as she finished reading. She was no closer to learning who might have stolen their trinoculars, and now she had even more questions that needed answering: why were the Adélie penguins diving so deep? And what on earth was BOI? She looked up from the page as Wally lumbered into the pod, carrying a large brush with soft bristles.

"Is that what you use to clean whale teeth?" Agnes asked.

"Not teeth, exactly," Wally replied. "Oksana is a young southern minke whale who's always getting plastic caught in her baleen. Here at the outpost we can help her get rid of it."

Baleen, Agnes knew, was a fringe of bristles on the inside of some whales' mouths, which they used to filter sea water for food.

Ripples appeared in the pool and a purple-grey whale head burst through the water, sending splashes over Agnes's thermal bodysuit. Oksana was at least five metres long (Agnes could see her tail poking outside the pod) and had smooth skin except for a distinctive ridge running from the tip of her snout to her blowhole.

"Hi, Oksana," Agnes said. "I'm Agent Gamble. Don't be alarmed, but I need to ask you a few questions. I'm investigating the tremors that are damaging the outpost."

"I don't mind at all," Oksana replied. She had a slow, melodious voice, which

Agnes found relaxing. "I get nervous having my baleen cleaned, so talking is a good distraction." She cleared her blowhole with a sad *pfft*. "My friend Hickory normally comes with me to these appointments but I haven't seen him for days."

"Is Hickory a minke whale too?" Agnes asked.

Oksana shook her head, sending water spilling out of the pool. "He's an Adélie penguin. I've been looking for him everywhere. He's normally easy to spot because he has unusual brown feathers."

An Adélie with brown feathers...

Agnes froze. "Oksana – I think I might have seen Hickory yesterday! Is he hard of hearing and not very talkative?"

Oksana's closest eye – which was the size of Agnes's fist – blinked. "No, that doesn't sound like Hickory. He's a real chatterbox. Normally I can't get a word in edgeways."

Frowning, Agnes jotted Oksana's description of Hickory into her "Field Notes" journal. "The brown penguin I saw was wearing a tracking device around his neck that looked like a silver bow tie, with a green flashing light in the middle. Was Hickory wearing one when—?"

But before Agnes could finish her question, Wally dropped his brush to the floor with a clang.

"A *silver bow tie with a green flashing light?*" he repeated. His hooves tapped anxiously against the floor. "Oh dear, oh dear. I came across a bowtie like that during my last **SPEARS** mission – it's not a tracking device at all! It's a gadget developed by enemies of **SPEARS** which uses forbidden jewel-wasp technology to control the mind of whoever is wearing it!"

Agnes went numb with shock. *A mind-control device...?* "That has to be why the Adélies are acting strangely," she realized, racing for the door. "They're under someone's control! I've got to tell Attie."

Oksana raised her flipper in farewell as Agnes and Wally left the dental pod and raced across the outpost building.

"Agent Attenborough was in the north wing a few minutes ago, interviewing a pregnant sea spider," Wally said as they ran. "I passed them on the way here."

When they got to the right pod, the door was open and the sea spider was trying to wriggle free from under a net ... but Attie was gone.

"They took him!" the sea spider cried. "It all happened so fast I didn't see who was who."

Agnes noticed a brown feather on the
floor and picked it up. Panic seized her chest
as she realized what had happened:
Attie had been shrew-napped!

CHAPTER SEVEN

Agnes, Rahul, Dita and Wally quickly took their seats around a table in the outpost briefing room. Agnes held up the brown feather so they could all see. "I found this in the pod where Attie was captured," she told them.

Dita cocked her head and examined the feather carefully, her eyeballs swivelling. "Penguin," she identified curtly.

Agnes nodded. "I think it might belong to a rare brown Adélie named Hickory. Steelsharp fitted bow ties to all the penguins in his colony, so *she* has to be the one controlling them; I just don't understand why she would order Hickory to shrew-nap Attie!" Agnes had gone over it again and again. Steelsharp was an animal lover; it didn't make sense.

Wally opened a laptop in the middle of the table. "This report might help explain things," he said gravely. "We received it from **SPEARS** HQ moments ago. Thank goodness Agent Attenborough fixed our communications equipment yesterday, or we would never have got it."

On the screen appeared three words: **TOP-SECRET INTELLIGENCE.**

Then, a short video began. It showed Cynthia Steelsharp with a harness strapped around her trademark tangerine-orange jacket, hanging from the side of a mountain as she filmed a documentary about harpy eagles. This was followed by a clip of Steelsharp in the same mountain location, using explosives to blast through the stone door of an ancient temple overgrown with vines. *"To most people,"* a voice-over announced, *"Cynthia Steelsharp is an award-winning documentary maker and rare-bird expert. However,* **SPEARS** *has discovered that she leads a double life."*

The video continued, showing clips of Steelsharp breaking into desert tombs, looting Aztec gold and raiding ancient burial sites.

"Steelsharp stops at nothing in her mercenary treasure looting, destroying the habitats of hundreds of plants and animals in her hunt for priceless artefacts," the voice-over went on, *"and, rather than donating her finds to museums, she auctions them off to the highest bidders – some of whom are known enemies of* **SPEARS***. She is considered highly dangerous."*

As the video finished, Agnes squeezed her fists, wishing she'd trusted her instincts sooner. Everything she'd seen in Steelsharp's tent – the polluting generator, the maps, the AUCTION-marked calendar – they all made sense now. "All this time we thought

Steelsharp was helping the environment when she was actually harming it," she said. She thought how disappointed Attie would be when he found out... If he hadn't already discovered the truth for himself, that is.

Rahul shook his head in disbelief. "I don't get it. There's no ancient treasure in Antarctica, so what's Steelsharp doing here?"

Ancient treasure... Something tugged at the back of Agnes's memory. She pulled the laptop over and typed *shipwreck* and *Antarctica* into the search bar, then raced through the results. "A colossal squid called Haruki told me that he often sleeps in an ancient shipwreck near by," she explained, running her finger across the screen. "Here it is. According to a historical study, a treasure galleon from southern Argentina sank during a storm hundreds of years ago. The shipwreck is buried in the ice, not too far from this outpost." She rifled back through her interview notes. "That could be why the Adélies are diving deeper than normal – perhaps Steelsharp has ordered them to search for the sunken ship?"

"I bet Steelsharp's got something to do with the tremors too," Rahul said, narrowing his eyes. "And your stolen trinoculars. It's too much of a coincidence otherwise."

Dita nodded quietly, looking thoughtful.

All of the clues seemed to be falling into place, except one.

"But ... I still don't understand why Steelsharp has taken Attie," Agnes admitted. Her heart clenched at the thought of her partner trapped and alone. If the situation was reversed and she was the one who had been kidnapped, she knew exactly what Attie would do. "I've got to rescue him," she announced, standing from the table, "*and* free the penguin colony from those awful devices. I'll deal with the tremors afterwards."

"In that case, I'm coming with you," Wally said, rising from his - rather large - chair.

"The thought of all those poor confused penguins makes my hooves shudder. We've got to save them."

"Well, you can't mount a rescue mission without me," Dita added, scurrying up onto Wally's back. "I want to help."

Rahul considered the three of them with a nervous smile. "Then the rescue team is assembled. I'll stay here to look after the outpost. Just ... be careful."

Out on the ice, Agnes pulled down her visor and started up the engine of the supersonic otter sled. She had a simple plan: infiltrate Steelsharp's camp, remove the mind-control bow ties from the penguins and search for Attie. "Hang on, everyone," she warned, "things are about to get *fast*."

She squeezed the accelerator and the sled rocketed forward. Wind roared all around them. Her ears popped as they hurtled over the ice, the Antarctic landscape flashing past in a blur of blue and white.

In order to keep the sled balanced,
she was riding up front, with Wally in the
middle, and Dita tucked on the back. It was
an especially ticklish arrangement as Wally's
horns kept poking Agnes's head, but it was
the only way the three of them could
fit on.

As they sped along, Agnes's thoughts
returned to Attie's shrew-napping. Only
registered patients and staff were allowed
aboard the outpost, so Hickory must have
had help from someone on the inside to gain
access. She swallowed as she realized there
really was a traitor in their midst...

"This is amazing!" Wally cried, gripping the sled handles.

Dita went to respond, but her long sticky tongue blew out of her mouth and got caught under her hood.

Agnes had never imagined it was possible to move so fast, but she couldn't enjoy the thrill of it without Attie by her side. Every time she thought about him being in trouble, her insides felt heavy.

Suddenly, a red warning light flashed on the dashboard and the sled slowed down.

"What's happening?" Wally asked.

Agnes checked the controls. "I'm not sure. The sled's dropped out of supersonic mode." Surveying their surroundings, she spotted a long blue crack tearing through the ice towards them. Her boots vibrated. "It's the tremors – they're happening again!"

The sled shook as the ground split and a huge crevasse opened beneath them. "Hold on!" Wally bellowed. Dita gave a panicked yelp as the vehicle went tumbling over the edge.

CHAPTER EIGHT

Everything seemed to happen in slow motion.
As they plummeted into the chasm, Wally
launched himself out of the sled head first
and plunged his horns into the icy crevasse
wall. Agnes hooked her arms around the sled
handles and clung on as the vehicle landed

with a jolt on a snowy ledge several metres down.

Gasping with relief, she turned around to find the back of the sled empty. "Dita! Where are you?"

"Down here!"

Agnes peered over the side of the sled. Dita was stranded on another ice shelf, much further down inside the chasm.

"I'm not hurt!" Dita called. "Just stuck."

While Agnes rummaged through her pack for a rope, Wally used his hooves like ice picks to climb to the surface and haul himself back out onto the ice.

His voice echoed as he yelled, "Once you've fetched Dita, tie your rope to the sled and throw the other end up here. That way, I can pull you both up."

But as Agnes lowered her rope towards Dita, her heart sank. It only reached halfway! She recalled her **SPEARS** training. With the correct equipment, she could safely climb down and rescue Dita, but all the gear she needed was back on the omnifrog.

"Don't worry about me," Dita shouted up. "I'll radio Rahul for help and wait here. Time's running out for you to save those penguins and stop Steelsharp!"

Agnes bit her lip, unsure what to do. She wished Attie was there. He had once told her that having to make tough decisions was part of being an agent; now she understood what he'd meant. "All right," Agnes agreed. "But will you radio us as soon as Rahul arrives, so we know you're OK?"

Dita promised that she would, and waved

goodbye to Agnes as Wally heaved the otter sled back to the surface. It was with a heavy heart that Agnes powered up the supersonic engine and she and Wally zoomed off, leaving Dita behind.

Soon enough, Steelsharp's tent appeared in the distance, surrounded by hundreds of abandoned penguin nests.

"Where do you think all the Adélies have gone?" Wally whispered as they crept towards the tent.

Agnes noticed how messy the penguins' nests were, as if the birds had all left in a hurry. "I don't know but we'd better stay alert." She flattened her ear against the tent canvas, but couldn't hear anything. After a glance in either direction, she slipped inside.

There were no lights on, so Agnes

scanned the shadows carefully.
Steelsharp's luxury velvet
sofas and deep-pile rugs were
soaking wet and covered with
penguin feathers. A stained-
glass lamp lay smashed
on the floor and several
books had fallen from
the shelves.
"Over there,"
Wally said, pointing.
"That looks like the
transmitter used
to control the bow
ties. We'll need to
destroy it to free
the penguins."

Agnes followed the direction of Wally's hoof towards the far corner of the tent, where a strange metal contraption flashed with green lights. Beneath it, something was *moving*.

Agnes squinted, and gasped. Attie was trussed up on the floor amongst Steelsharp's antiques! His four legs had been bound together with rope and there was a mouldy satsuma stuffed in his mouth.

"*Mmm!*"
he mumbled,
when he saw Agnes.
"*Mmm. Mmm.*"

"Don't worry," she called. "Everything's
going to be all right."

But as she took a step forward, hundreds
of pairs of penguin eyes flicked open in the
darkness. There were Adélies huddled behind
chairs and hunched under tables; crammed
between antiques and hidden inside boxes ...
and the green lights on their bow ties were
flashing furiously.

"Look out!" Wally yelled. "It's a trap!"

Without warning, one
penguin leaped from
a bookshelf and aimed
a kick towards Agnes,

who lurched aside just in time. The penguin landed on a sofa and wobbled upright with a dazed look on its face. "Terribly sorry about that," it said. "I can't seem to control my—" It suddenly struck a ninja pose with its wings. "Oh dear. I think I'm going to attack you again!"

As Agnes darted out of the way, three more penguins charged.

"I must apologize!"

"Do forgive me."

"Oh, bother!"

Wally barrelled forwards, knocking the birds over like bowling pins. "I'll try to keep them busy," he told Agnes. "You free Agent Attenborough and destroy the transmitter. Go!"

Agnes squeezed her fists together and focused on Attie. No penguin assault course was going to stop her from rescuing her partner.

Advancing across the tent, she ducked to avoid a penguin swinging from the roof and slid past several more practising kung fu. Adélies jumped out at her from all directions, offering apologies.

"Dreadfully sorry!" one called as it aimed a punch at her knee.

"Please excuse us!" begged another, mid-sliding tackle.

One bird started throwing antique cricket balls at Agnes to try to trip her up, but she managed to keep her balance and hop over them. Finally reaching the other side of the tent, she threw a glance over her shoulder

to check on Wally, who
looked like a giant
hairy Christmas
tree dangling with
penguin baubles.

Attie was now only
metres away, but there
was one last penguin
standing guard with its flippers folded.
It had a confused look on its face and its
brown feathers were ruffled.

Hickory. Agnes was relieved to see that
the missing penguin was safe; but she also
needed to find a way past him.

Remembering her training in the secret
fighting style of animai-tai, she drew her
legs apart and stretched her arms above
her head. She needed to temporarily disable

Hickory without hurting him, and there was only one move she knew that might work: the flutter-moth cub-hug.

Bending her knees, she jumped up high and then dived, flapping her arms towards Hickory. She brought her hands down at just the right angle on either side of his body and squeezed gently.

The result was immediate: both of Hickory's flippers went to sleep. He swayed on the spot, unable to stay balanced without them, and fell onto his tummy.

With no time to spare, Agnes vaulted over Hickory, followed the transmitter's power cable and switched the device off at the socket. The green light on Hickory's bow tie flickered before going dark.

Hickory blinked and rubbed his head.

"Erg," he groaned. "Why do I have such a headache?"

"Everything's going to be OK," Agnes reassured him, stroking his shoulder gently. "We're from **SPEARS** and we're going to help you feel better, I promise."

All around the tent, the lights on the Adélies' bow ties had stopped flashing. The penguins that had been attacking Wally slithered down his body and formed a feathery mound on the floor.

"It's all right," Wally said, helping the penguins up. "You've been through quite an ordeal, but you're going to be fine."

With the colony being cared for, Agnes hurried over to Attie, removed the saliva-covered satsuma from his mouth and untied his ropes. "Are you OK?"

"I feel like such a silly shrew," he said, crinkling his long nose. "I should have listened to you. Your instincts were right about Steelsharp. She isn't the person I thought she was. And a *satsuma*! The shame of it!" As the last of the ropes fell to the floor, he stood staring at his feet. "I'm sorry. I wasn't a very good partner, or friend."

Unable to stop herself, Agnes scooped Attie into her arms and hugged him fiercely against her chest. "You're the best partner! I was so worried about you."

"I knew you'd find me," Attie said, his voice slightly muffled as he wriggled out of her grasp and dropped to the floor in a crouch. "But now we need to hurry. I've discovered what's causing the tremors!" He guided her through the crowd of recovering penguins to a desk in the opposite corner of the tent. Spread on top of it was a blueprint for a specially adapted submarine with a huge propeller at one end and a drill-head covered in jagged metal teeth at the other.

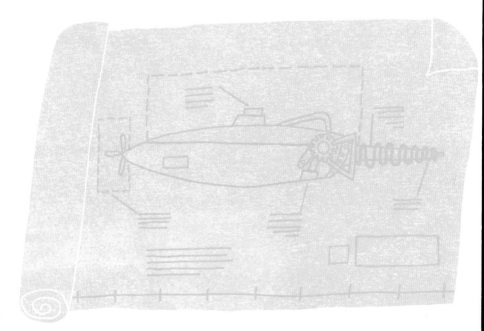

Agnes read the title with dismay: *Mammoth Drill-Deep Icicle Submarine.*

"Steelsharp made the Adélies construct this submarine for her," Attie said. Agnes studied the details of the diagram carefully. The submarine appeared to be designed for burrowing into the ice. "It's so powerful that every time Steelsharp uses it, it causes shockwaves which reverberate for miles around. She put one of those ghastly bow ties around my neck to force me to tell her how to use the trinoculars, so she could look for something that's buried in the ice and drill it out."

"That's why she captured you," Agnes realized. "She couldn't use the trinoculars without you." She shared with Attie what she'd learned about the sunken treasure galleon.

"I've memorized its co-ordinates."

He gave her a satisfied nod. "That's it! That's what she's looking for. If we head for those co-ordinates, we should find Steelsharp and the submarine." His whiskers twitched. "There's something else. I overheard Steelsharp talking about her *assistant* aboard the outpost. Whoever they are, *they* stole the trinoculars."

Agnes got a horrible sinking feeling in her stomach. Their suspicions had been correct: there was a traitor in their midst.

"The penguins are all suffering from extreme dizziness," Wally said, lumbering over. "And they've got horrendous headaches. I need to get the entire colony back to the outpost as soon as possible."

Agnes looked at Attie and knew he

was thinking the same as her: the outpost building would very soon be full with patients, which meant they needed to stop Steelsharp using the Mammoth Drill-Deep Icicle Submarine *now*. "You can borrow the omnifrog," she told Wally. "If the colony can all fit inside this tent, they should be able to squeeze on there. Attie and I will stop Steelsharp."

From under the hood of his thermal bodysuit, Attie gazed up at her. "Right you are, partner."

Since he didn't have time to argue, Agnes planted Attie on her shoulder and together they trekked as quickly as possible back to the water.

Attie's long tail curled around Agnes's neck as he clung on. "I'm hatching a plan," he said in her ear, "but in order for it to work we'll need to be able to get close to the drill without Steelsharp noticing."

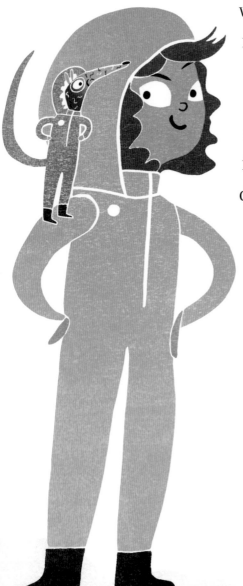

Agnes thought back to her **SPEARS** training in the art of disguise. She had an idea...

CHAPTER NINE

Deep underwater, Agnes found herself
floating with her arms stretched alongside
her body, encased in a long, slimy costume.
She and Attie had stitched the outfit together
from pieces of giant Antarctic seaweed which
was thick, brown and rubbery, and perfect for
imitating the skin of one particular creature:
a southern elephant seal.

"If the co-ordinates are correct, we should be able to see Steelsharp soon," Attie said, down at Agnes's feet. He was operating the seal's tail, while Agnes had control of the seal's head. They had to work in perfect unison for the seal's movements to look natural. "Bear left twenty-five degrees," he directed.

Agnes pitched her body left, shimmied her hips to activate the seal's flippers, and they were away. Peering through the visor of her watertight thermal bodysuit, she looked out through the seal's mouth. Hardly any light penetrated this far down in the ocean. It was a dark, mysterious place. The built-in breathing apparatus in her bodysuit buzzed quietly as they glided forward.

Just then, lights flickered in the

distance. Agnes tensed as the serrated drill-head of the Mammoth Drill-Deep Icicle Submarine emerged out of the shadows. It was bigger and spikier than the blueprint had suggested, and with a shiver Agnes spotted Steelsharp strapped inside the cockpit, holding the stolen trinoculars to her eyes. Behind the sub, the bow of an old seaweed-covered ship jutted from a wall of ice. Agnes could just about see the outline of the rest of the treasure galleon buried behind it.

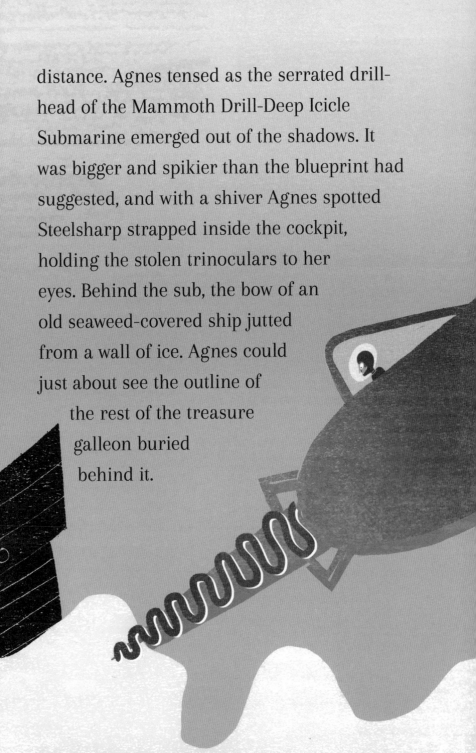

"According to those blueprints, we can disable the drill by pulling a lever located inside the control panel at the base of Steelsharp's submarine," Attie said. He flicked the seal's tail, giving them a turn of speed and they zoomed forward. Agnes held her breath as Steelsharp lowered the trinoculars and turned to look in their direction...

Steelsharp's eyes narrowed. But, seeing only a gormless elephant seal splashing by, she turned away.

Phew, Agnes sighed, although her pulse was still racing. With a wiggle of her body, she sent the elephant seal diving under the submarine until they were in position below the control panel. "OK, time to shake off this disguise," she told Attie. She tucked her knees into her chest and drove her feet down hard,

bursting out of the seal costume through a flap in its tummy.

"We've got to hurry," Attie urged, escaping via a hole in the seal's tail. He handed Agnes a screwdriver. "Steelsharp could notice us at any moment."

Agnes hadn't practised underwater mechanics before, so she had to concentrate hard to unfasten the control panel. Once inside, she discovered a row of six different-coloured levers. "Which one do I pull?"

Attie's long nose flicked to and fro as he considered their choices. "I don't know; this wasn't on the blueprints!"

Agnes thought back to her **SPEARS** training with Aristophanes. With time running out, she summoned her courage and yanked on the purple lever. Rather than shutting down the drill, it sent the submarine's rear propeller spinning in reverse, drawing water towards it.

Attie had to swim frantically to avoid being sucked in. "It's definitely not that one!"

Agnes pushed the purple lever back to its original position and tugged on the red one. This time, there was a loud clanking noise as the submarine's propeller jarred to a halt. Three bubbles rose like hot-air balloons from the rear of the vessel, but the lights in the cockpit remained on, with the drill engine still whirring.

"That must be the wrong one, too!" Attie fretted. "What about—?" But before he could finish his sentence, he disappeared in a cloud of bubbles. Agnes's skin went cold as she heard an amplified angry voice over her shoulder.

"I should have known you two would be trouble."

She spun around to find Steelsharp swimming closer to her, dressed in a tangerine-orange diving suit and helmet with built-in microphone. In one hand she clutched Attie by the scruff of his neck; in the other she held a harpoon – a horrible weapon with a barbed spear on the end that attached

to a long rope.

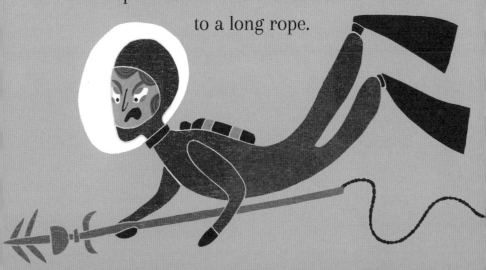

"You **SPEARS** agents
are all the same," Steelsharp
snarled. "Always poking your
noses into other people's business."
She tightened her grip on Attie, who was
wriggling desperately to get free. "Now,
unless you want your partner to have more
holes than a fishing net, I suggest you move
away from that control panel!"

Agnes tensed, unsure what to do. Attie was in danger, but if Steelsharp used the drill again, the entire outpost might be destroyed.

"We know what you're really up to, Steelsharp!" Attie cried bravely. "We won't let you damage any more habitats in your search for treasure!"

Steelsharp laughed. "And how exactly do you plan on stopping us? "

Us? Agnes wasn't sure what Steelsharp meant, until she spotted a small four-legged creature emerge from the cockpit of the submarine and come swimming towards them...

"*Dita?*" Agnes drew her breath. The chameleon was wielding a harpoon like Steelsharp's. "I thought you were trapped in the crevasse!"

Dita sniggered. "No, I had my own escape plan. I only let you *believe* I was trapped, just like I let you believe I was poor, panicked *Dita*. In actual fact, my name is Slink."

Staring aghast at Dita – or rather, Slink – Agnes pieced the clues together. "*You're* the one who's been helping Steelsharp," Agnes said, her body going limp with shock. "You stole the trinoculars and helped Hickory shrew-nap Attie!"

"That's right," Slink said, her eyes glinting with pride. "My camouflage comes in handy when I have to sneak around. Cynthia recognized my talents when I was a hatchling and trained me to be a treasure-hunter, like her." She pointed her harpoon at Agnes. "Now, get away from our submarine!"

Edging
backwards, Agnes
felt the hull of
the submarine
press against her
shoulders. There
was no escape. She
looked in all directions,
trying to think of a way out,
and suddenly remembered the control panel
was still open. Quick as a flash, she reached
round and wrenched on the purple lever.

With a loud whir, the propeller at the rear
of the submarine began churning in reverse,
dragging everything towards it.

"Wha—?" Slink spluttered, trying to
swim away. As she was pulled towards the
propeller, she fired her harpoon into the ice

around the treasure galleon.
The rope uncoiled with a loud
WHOOOSH and Slink held on
tight, dangling from the end.
Steelsharp floundered, trying to keep
a grip on Attie. Eventually she had to release
him so she too could shoot her harpoon and
hang onto the ice wall.

With both spears lodged in the ice, Agnes
had a brainwave. She pushed the purple
lever back in place and swam over to Attie.
"Can you lure Slink clockwise around the
sub while I get Steelsharp to follow me anti-
clockwise? I have an idea."

Attie nodded and, following Agnes's
instructions, blew a raspberry in Slink's

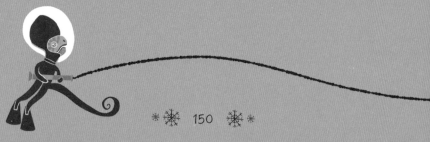

direction. "If you want that treasure, you'll have to catch us!" he taunted, zooming off. Slink turned an angry shade of red and dived after him, still holding her harpoon.

Steelsharp glowered at Agnes. "This will be the first and last time **SPEARS** interferes with our business, I promise you." With the harpoon tucked under her arm, she kicked her flippers and came towards Agnes.

Agnes swam away as fast as she could, looping around the submarine in the opposite direction to Attie. Steelsharp and Slink pursued them, but with every orbit, their harpoon ropes got shorter and tighter. Before they had realized what was happening, they were tangled up in a rope knot.

They both let go of their harpoons, but it was too late.

"What the—?!" Slink spluttered, turning every colour of the rainbow as she tried to squirm free.

"Argh, get this off me!" Steelsharp yelled, writhing furiously in an attempt to slither out from under the harpoon ropes. But too many loops of the submarine had wound the ropes tightly, leaving Steelsharp and Slink tied around the submarine like the ribbons on a present.

Eventually, both she and Slink gave up the struggle. There was no way they'd escape now.

Attie gave Agnes an underwater high-five and then looked stonily at Steelsharp. "To think I ever admired you!" he exclaimed. "Your days of destruction are over; you will

never harm another animal or plant
habitat again. The justice department
at **SPEARS** will see to that!"

CHAPTER TEN

Sometime later in the outpost briefing room,
Agnes tapped her fingers against the table.
Beside her, Attie's tail swung side to side.
"Any minute now," he said, staring at the
laptop screen. "Commander Phil is always
punctual."

"What do you think he'll say?" Agnes asked. "He must have read the whole mission report by now."

"I don't know," Attie said, nervously. "Our partnership has been tested. He's going to have a few questions."

Just then the screen flickered and an image appeared. Commander Phil was sitting in his office at **SPEARS** HQ with a paper file on his desk. On the front were the words: *OPERATION ICEBEAK: MISSION REPORT.* "It seems Antarctica was a tough challenge," he said, gruffly. "Shrew-napping, false identities, accidents on the ice..."

Agnes's shoulders sank, thinking of all the things that had gone wrong. If only she hadn't fallen into that crevasse, or they'd uncovered Slink's real identity sooner...

"Tell me, what do you think was your

most important mistake?"

Attie shared a confused glance with Agnes. "Our most *important* mistake? It's difficult to say, sir," he answered. "I'm afraid we made quite a few."

Replaying the question in her mind, Agnes realized something. "*All* our mistakes were important," she said. "It's only by learning from them that we can become better **SPEARS** agents."

The Commander's beak split into a grin. "That's right!" he declared, clapping his wings together. "The ability to learn from your own – and each other's – mistakes is the sign of a true partnership. If missions always went smoothly, we'd never learn to be quick-thinking field agents, would we? And with another *successful* mission under your belt, you two are stronger than ever, if you ask me!"

Outside, the puddled corridors of the outpost were buzzing with activity. A babble of chatter drifted through the air as all manner of feathered, scaled, shelled and tentacled wildlife scuttled, waddled and slithered to and fro. Even allowing for the addition of an entire colony of Adélie penguins, there were suddenly far more animals in the outpost than Agnes remembered there being before. Something was happening...

"The Adélies are recovering well," Attie commented, peeking into a treatment pod. Agnes looked over his head. The room contained several Adélie penguins wrapped in snuggly bathrobes, relaxing on stone loungers. She sighed deeply, glad they didn't appear to be suffering any lasting side-effects from their ordeal.

Footsteps clattered along the corridor. "You saved the outpost!" Rahul cried, charging towards them. "Thank you both so much!" He gave Agnes a hug and patted Attie on the head, causing him to cross his arms in protest. "Now we can repair all the damage caused by the tremors, without fear that they will happen again."

"And all the important work we're doing here will continue," Wally added, lumbering up behind him.

Attie stood a little straighter, lifting his chest proudly. "Well, we couldn't have done it without you two. It's true what they say: you're never alone when you're part of the **SPEARS** family."

Agnes got a warm feeling inside as she understood that Attie was right. Being a part of **SPEARS** meant she had friends all around her – even in a remote place like Antarctica.

All at once, the noise in the corridor hushed. There was a shuffle of movement at the far end and then two **SPEARS** guards appeared around the corner with Cynthia Steelsharp and Slink trudging between them. Steelsharp's copper hair hung limply over the

shoulders of a drab grey uniform that had the words *OCEAN CLEAN-UP* printed on the back. Slink was dressed in a similarly dreary outfit.

"What will happen to them?" Agnes asked, watching the guards escort Steelsharp and Slink into another omnifrog.

"They'll be put to work gathering plastic rubbish from our oceans," Wally explained with a shrug. "It's a fitting punishment if you ask me."

Agnes nodded but she knew it would take more than vanquishing Steelsharp and Slink to protect Antarctica. Most of the outpost's treatment pods were occupied; there was still a long way to go to save the plants and animals that called this incredible part of the world home.

"Have you heard about the treasure galleon?" Rahul asked. "A specialist conservation team are on their way here now to safely excavate the artefacts on board and donate them to a museum in Argentina, where the ship originally came from. The starfish said they might see if they can use the wreck as a hotel afterwards!"

Before Agnes could respond, a sea snail came sliding down the hallway at an alarming speed. "It's them!" the snail cried. "BOI! They're here!"

BOI? Agnes glanced worriedly at Attie. They'd heard those letters before. "Do you know what that means?" she whispered.

"Of course!" Wally and Rahul replied simultaneously. They each unzipped the top half of their thermal bodysuits to reveal

T-shirts printed with photos of a gang of penguins holding microphones.

"BOI stands for *Beaks On Ice*," Rahul explained. "They're the world's only seven-species penguin band, all former **SPEARS** agents."

"And they've just arrived here on the Antarctic stop of their world tour!" Wally added, excitedly.

Rahul checked his watch. "The concert is about to start. Are you coming?"

A short time later, Agnes and Attie – dressed in their thermal bodysuits – found themselves treading water in the Southern Ocean, surrounded by a crowd of marine animals. A jagged iceberg towered over them all.

Halfway up, a shelf had been cut into the ice and a curtain of bioluminescent starfish hung behind it, glowing brightly in the dark evening air.

It was a spectacular stage, and there were seven spectacular penguins standing in a line upon it. They ranged in size from a tiny Galápagos penguin, to a huge emperor penguin. Two of the species – a rockhopper and a macaroni – had striking yellow feathers above their eyes, and one – a fairy penguin – had beautiful blue eyes and feathers. Agnes noticed they were all wearing **SPEARS** communication pins.

"Hello, Antarctica!" one of the penguins – a chubby black and white Chinstrap – shouted. "Are you ready to rock?"

The crowd roared. Some held up banners

that read, "*WE LOVE BEAKS ON ICE*" and
"*BOI ARE THE BEST!*" Agnes spotted a
reunited Oksana and Hickory, slapping their
flippers against the surface of the water and
cheering. Haruki was waving his tentacles in
the air with a rainbow-wide smile on his face.

A crackle emitted from two large seaweed speakers at the side of the stage, and then BOI started singing:

"*If you wanna swim in my ocean,*
If you wanna be in my colony,
Gotta feed us no pollution,
Gotta keep us plastic-free..."

The water swelled with waves as everyone danced and sang along. Attie grinned and pointed to the bulbous grey head of an

elephant seal, bobbing up and down in the crowd. "Looks like someone's found a friend."

Agnes squinted and recognized the large elephant seal she'd foolishly traded their bananas with yesterday. Only ... he wasn't alone. He was dancing with another seal who had very saggy brown, seaweed-textured skin. She giggled as she realized – it was their old costume!

"Would you like to dance?" Attie said, offering Agnes his paw.

She beamed. "Absolutely!"

As they boogied in the water – Attie swishing his tail and Agnes shaking her hips – she considered what an incredible journey they'd been on together. She knew exactly what she'd write in her "Field Notes" when she got back to the omnifrog:

OPERATION ICEBEAK

by Agnes Gamble (**SPEARS** Field Agent)

UPDATE:

Operation Icebeak has been a success! Agent Attenborough and I saved the outpost, freed a colony of penguins and uncovered an enemy spy. We also made some new friends in **SPEARS** and I got to visit the incredible Antarctic landscape that my parents explored. My partnership with Agent Attenborough is getting stronger. I only wonder where our next adventure will take us...

OBSERVATIONS:

* Not all chameleons can be trusted.
* Never come between a shrew and his favourite sandwich.
* No one rocks an iceberg like BOI.

OPERATION: ICEBEAK

MISSION TYPE:	AID & INVESTIGATE
SPECIES NAME:	ADÉLIE PENGUINS

PYGOSCELIS ADELIAE (SCIENTIFIC)

ASSIGNED EQUIPMENT:

OMNIFROG, TRINOCULARS,
SUPERSONIC OTTER SLED,
TELESCOPIC GIRAFFE-STILTS

SECURITY CLASSIFICATION:

TOP SECRET

AGENT ATTENBOROUGH AND AGENT GAMBLE TO BE
DEPLOYED TO ANTARCTICA FOR OPERATION: ICEBEAK

CASE FILE NUMBER: 02104199505

TOP SECRET

CONFIDENTIAL

SPEARS OFFICIAL

COMMUNICATION

TOP SECRET	096
SECURITY CLASSIFICATION:	MISSION NO.

Dear Reader,

It's Commander Phil again, calling all **SPEARS** agents!

As you may know, Agents Attenborough and Gamble have just completed a mission in Antarctica – the highest, driest, windiest and coldest continent on Earth. Unfortunately, the fragile Antarctic ecosystem is under threat and needs our protection.

Why is Antarctica important?

Most of Antarctica lies within the Antarctic Circle, an imaginary line that circles the southern part of the Earth. Almost all of the land there is covered by a thick layer of ice that slides around, forming glaciers and huge ice shelves that float on the sea. These are home to a unique variety of seals, penguins and other seabirds. The waters around Antarctica also support a vast array of sea life, including whales, dolphins, fish and *plankton* - an important food source for many other ocean creatures. Antarctica's white ice reflects some of the sun's rays back into space, helping to regulate the Earth's temperature. Now that's *cool*!

What's the problem?

Human activity is releasing more and more carbon dioxide into the Earth's atmosphere, causing the planet to heat up. This effect is called *global warming* and the Antarctic Peninsula is warming faster than anywhere else on Earth. Animals are losing their homes and breeding grounds because the glaciers are melting. In the Southern Ocean, Antarctic wildlife is also being threatened by illegal fishing. Long lines and hooks trap seabirds, and fishing boats cause injuries to whales and dolphins. Plastic is polluting the water. Seabirds are eating it by mistake and whales can get it caught in their baleens, preventing them from feeding.

WHO'S IN DANGER?

With hurricane-force winds and temperatures as low as -60ºC, Antarctica is a harsh and unforgiving habitat. That's why the animals that live there are specially adapted to survive. Some have thick skin or a layer of insulating fur to keep them warm. Others, like the Antarctic Silverfish, produce their own antifreeze. Even so, many species are at risk:

WANDERING ALBATROSS

The Wandering Albatross has the largest wingspan of any living bird.

It is capable of remaining in the air for several hours without flapping its wings.

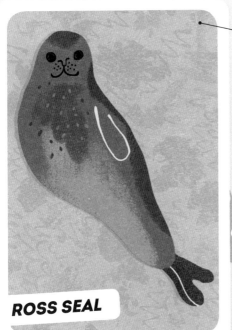

ROSS SEAL

The Ross Seal has short fur and disproportionately large eyes, and can make an underwater "siren" noise that can be heard long distances away.

A small species of whale that feeds on krill and can survive up to 50 years in the wild.

ANTARCTIC MINKE WHALE

This seabird is sooty-black with a white throat and chin. It leaves Antarctica to breed on several subtropical islands in the South Atlantic Ocean.

WHITE-CHINNED PETREL

The small and feisty Adélie Penguin can hold its breath for up to 6 minutes, and dive as deep as 180 metres underwater!

ADÉLIE PENGUIN

CRITICALLY ENDANGERED

EMPEROR PENGUIN

Emperor Penguins can grow to over 115cm tall – that's taller than the average six-year-old!

Once they've laid their eggs, the male looks after them while the female goes to find food.

The Fin Whale has a long, slender body with a pale underside and is the second largest species of whale on Earth.

A newborn Fin Whale is already over 6 metres in length!

FIN WHALE

OMNIFROG

TRAVEL ROUTE

JOURNEY TO ANTARCTICA

UNCLE DOUGLAS'S APARTMENT

SCOTIA SEA

SPEARS OUTPOST

SCOTIA SEA

WEDDELL S

FINISH

ANTARCTICA

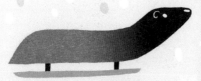
SUPERSONIC OTTER SLED

START

168 HOUR JOURNEY
UNDER THE SEA

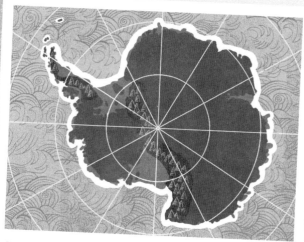
ANTARCTIC PENINSULA

OPERATION: ICEBEAK

Get to know your carbon footprint!

Everyone has a carbon footprint. It is the amount of carbon dioxide that is released into the air because of your energy needs. When you ride in a car, switch on a light or even eat a beef burger, you are adding to your footprint. The good news is, there are lots of easy ways to reduce your footprint and help lower global warming.

Switch off and get walking!

Our homes are powered by energy generated by burning fossil fuels, which release carbon dioxide. You can conserve energy by switching off lights and appliances when you're not using them, and shutting the doors in your house to keep in the warmth. Cars also burn fossil fuels, so next time you travel to school or round to your friend's house, why not walk, bike, skateboard or rollerblade to get there?

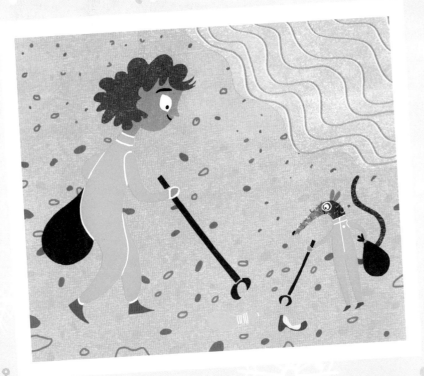

Host a beach clean-up day!

Plastic is *not* fantastic. When we dispose of it, it makes its way into the oceans and is often mistaken for food by birds and sea life. You can help by recycling plastic packaging and donating any unwanted plastic toys to charity, to be reused. If you live near the sea, why not consider hosting a beach clean-up day? Get together with friends and family, and gather up any litter you find to prevent it from being washed into the ocean.

Be ocean-friendly!

Illegal fishing depletes fish stocks and harms wildlife. When you or your parents buy seafood, check that it is certified as sustainable by the MSC, the Marine Stewardship Council. This means it is caught in a way that doesn't have a negative impact on the environment.

Get creative in the kitchen!

Eating meat increases your carbon footprint, so if you enjoy cooking, why not try creating some tasty meat-free meals for your family and friends? You can find easy vegetarian or vegan recipes in books and online. Agent Attenborough insists that pumpkin-seed-and-fried-banana sandwiches are amazing, but I'm not so sure…

Good luck, agents!
SPEARS is relying on you.

Sincerely,

Commander Phil

JENNIFER BELL

Londoner Jennifer Bell worked as a children's bookseller and piranha-keeper at a world-famous bookshop before becoming an author. Her debut novel, *The Uncommoners: The Crooked Sixpence* was an international bestseller. **Agents of the Wild** is her first series for younger readers. She was recruited into **SPEARS** by a giant hairy armadillo named Maurice.

ALICE LICKENS

Co-creator Alice Lickens is an illustrator and author and a winner of the prestigious Sendak Fellowship for illustration. Her picture books include *Can You Dance to the Boogaloo?*, *How To Be A Cowboy*, and the Explorer activity book series with the National Trust. She joined **SPEARS** after receiving a tap on the shoulder from a Norwegian rat named Lorita.

Join
AGENTS OF THE WILD
on their first mission:

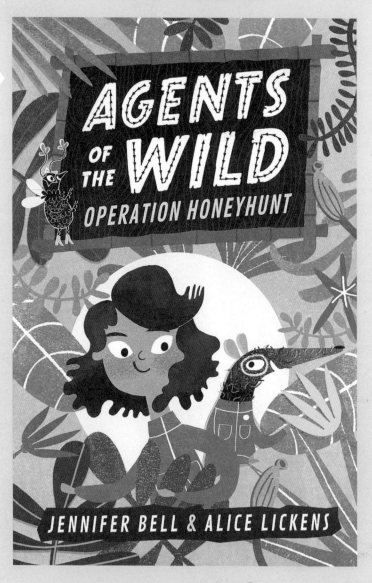

AGENTS
OF
THE WILD
OPERATION HONEYHUNT

JENNIFER BELL & ALICE LICKENS

Species in danger?
Girl and shrew to the rescue!